2008

The
Tiara
Club

✦ AT SILVER TOWERS ✦

The Tiara Club

Princess Charlotte *and the* Birthday Ball

Princess Katie *and the* Silver Pony

Princess Daisy *and the* Dazzling Dragon

Princess Sophia *and the* Sparkling Surprise

Princess Alice *and the* Magical Mirror

Princess Emily *and the* Substitute Fairy

———◆———

The Tiara Club at Silver Towers

Princess Charlotte *and the* Enchanted Rose

Princess Daisy *and the* Magical Merry-Go-Round

Princess Alice *and the* Glass Slipper

Princess Sophia *and the* Prince's Party

Princess Emily *and the* Wishing Star

~ VIVIAN FRENCH ~

The Tiara Club

✦ AT SILVER TOWERS ✦

Princess Katie
~ AND THE ~
Mixed-up Potion

ILLUSTRATED BY SARAH GIBB

KATHERINE TEGEN BOOKS
HarperTrophy®
An Imprint of HarperCollinsPublishers

Harper Trophy® is a registered trademark of
HarperCollins Publishers.

The Tiara Club at Silver Towers: Princess Katie
and the Mixed-up Potion
Text copyright © 2007 by Vivian French
Illustrations copyright © 2007 by Sarah Gibb

Library of Congress Cataloging-in-Publication Data
French, Vivian.
Princess Katie and the mixed-up potion / by Vivian French ;
illustrated by Sarah Gibb. — 1st U.S. ed.
p.   cm. — (The Tiara Club at Silver Towers)
Summary: Princess Katie and her classmates go on an outing
to a witch's house, where they learn about more than just mak-
ing magic potions.
ISBN-13: 978-0-06-112443-3 — ISBN-10: 0-06-112443-5
[1. Princesses—Fiction. 2. Witches—Fiction. 3. Magic—
Fiction. 4. Kindness—Fiction. 5. Schools—Fiction.] I. Gibb,
Sarah, ill. II. Title.
PZ7.F88917Prkm 2007   2006036263
[Fic]—dc22   CIP
AC

Typography by Amy Ryan
❖
First U.S. edition, 2007

For Princess Judith Elliott,
with love and admiration
—V.F.

For Rosa,
thanks for all your help
—S.G.

The Royal Palace Academy
for the Preparation of Perfect Princesses
(Known to our students as "The Princess Academy")

OUR SCHOOL MOTTO:
A Perfect Princess always thinks of others before herself,
and is kind, caring, and truthful.

Silver Towers offers a complete education for
Tiara Club princesses with emphasis on
selected outings. The curriculum includes:

Fans and Curtseys

A visit to Witch Windlespin
(Royal herbalist, healer, and maker of magic potions)

Problem Prime Ministers

A visit to the Museum of Royal Life
(Students will be well protected from the Poisoned Apple)

Our principal, Queen Samantha Joy, is present
at all times, and students are in the excellent care of
the school Fairy Godmother, Fairy Angora.

OUR RESIDENT STAFF & VISITING EXPERTS INCLUDE:

LADY ALBINA MacSPLINTER *(School Secretary)*
CROWN PRINCE DANDINO *(Field Trips)*
QUEEN MOTHER MATILDA *(Etiquette, Posture, and Poise)*
FAIRY G. *(Head Fairy Godmother)*

We award tiara points to encourage our
Tiara Club princesses toward the next level.
All princesses who win enough points at Silver
Towers will attend the Silver Ball, where they
will be presented with their Silver Sashes.

Silver Sash Tiara Club princesses are invited
to return to Ruby Mansions, our exclusive
residence for Perfect Princesses, where they may
continue their education at a higher level.

PLEASE NOTE:

Princesses are expected to arrive
at the Academy with a *minimum* of:

TWENTY BALL GOWNS
(with all necessary hoops,
petticoats, etc.)

TWELVE DAY-DRESSES

SEVEN GOWNS
suitable for garden parties
and other special daytime
occasions

TWELVE TIARAS

DANCING SHOES
five pairs

VELVET SLIPPERS
three pairs

RIDING BOOTS
two pairs

Cloaks, muffs, stoles, gloves,
and other essential
accessories, as required

Hello, and how are you? Thank you so much for being at Silver Towers with us. Oh! You do know who we are, don't you? I'm Princess Katie, and I share the Silver Rose Room with the Princesses Charlotte, Alice, Emily, Daisy, and Sophia. We're all trying really hard to earn our Silver Sashes, but it's a lot of work getting Tiara Points—especially when those awful twins are around.

Chapter One

"Gruella darling, could you ask Daisy to pass the marmalade? Nobody here has *any* manners, even though they're supposed to be princesses!"

We were sitting having our breakfast, and as usual the twins were showing off. Princess Diamonde was close enough to the marmalade she could easily have reached it herself.

I looked at Daisy, and she was staring at her plate. She didn't seem to have heard Diamonde at all. Alice leaned across the table and thumped the jar down, right under Diamonde's nose.

"Your marmalade, Your Majesty," she said.

"Sorry to have troubled you, I'm sure," Diamonde said in a nasty voice, and tipped at least half the jar onto her toast.

Sophia was sitting next to Daisy, and she'd noticed how quiet she was too.

"Are you all right?" she asked.

Daisy shook her head.

At once we all clustered around her, asking what was wrong. Daisy is so nice, and she's so kind, none of us wanted her to be unhappy.

"It's the school outing," Daisy said, and she sounded very nervous.

"I don't want to go. I'm scared!"

"What outing?" I asked. I hadn't heard about any outings, but I'm not always very good at remembering to read what's on our bulletin board. I certainly hadn't that morning, as I'd only just been in time for breakfast.

Emily and I had seen a row of coaches crossing the courtyard with the most beautiful horses, so of course we just *had* to sneak out and watch, and then the bell rang and we'd had to rush back in.

"Oh dear," said a loud voice behind me. "You mean you haven't heard that we're going to meet a *witch*?" Princess Gruella sniggered.

"Maybe you could ask for a spell to make Daisy more brave!" And she flounced away, cackling at her own joke, just as if she were a witch herself.

I ignored her and grabbed Charlotte. "Are we really going to meet a witch?"

Charlotte nodded, her eyes shining. "It was on the board this morning! Fairy Angora's taking us! We're going to spend the afternoon with Witch Windlespin, and hear about Good Magic"—and exactly at that moment, Crown Prince Dandino bounced into the breakfast hall, followed by Lady Albina, the school secretary. Prince Dandino's in charge of arranging field trips, and he was looking very excited, but Lady Albina seemed to be very glum.

Alice chuckled in my ear. "My big sis told me Lady Albina hates field trips," she whispered. "She thinks we'll all get lost!"

"Now, my dear young princesses," Prince Dandino said, "we have such a very special treat for you today. As you may know, Queen Samantha Joy thinks it is a very good thing for you to see how other people live their lives"—he stopped for a second to give Lady Albina a superior look—"and Witch Windlespin has very kindly offered to show you her beautiful home. The coaches will be leaving immediately after lunch, so please be ready. Fairy Angora will meet you at the main door at two o'clock precisely—don't be late!" And he bounced away.

Lady Albina sniffed disapprovingly. "If you look at the board you will find out which coach you are traveling in," she snapped. "And please make sure you wear your name tags and do exactly as you're told!"

As Lady Albina stalked out of the breakfast hall, I gave Daisy a hug, and Emily, Charlotte, Alice, and Sophia did too.

"You'll be fine!" I told her. "What could happen when you've got *us* to look after you?"

Then Daisy looked so much happier as we went to get our coats.

Chapter Two

We hadn't been on any outings before—well, only on very special occasions, like the time we flew on a dragon to King Percival's Celebration. It felt strange to be going away from Silver Towers that afternoon.

There was another coach in front of us, and two more behind. Luckily, we'd managed to avoid Gruella and Diamonde. They were in the last coach, which they weren't very happy about at all.

"Where do you think Witch Windlespin lives?" I asked Charlotte.

"I don't know," she said. "I hope it's not a dark creepy cave full of spiders!"

"I know!" Alice interrupted. "She lives in the middle of Hollyberry Wood, and she's famous for her magic cures. She does spinning and weaving as well, and her house is full of wonderful cushions and rugs and stuff. She makes her own clothes too, in the most fabulous colors."

"She makes clothes?" Emily sounded amazed. "That doesn't sound very witchy!"

"I thought witches always wore black," Charlotte said. "With pointy hats."

Daisy nodded. "Me too. And they have warts on their noses, and whiskers on their chins. And they put terrible spells on princesses!"

"Queen Samantha Joy would never let us go near anyone like

that," Sophia pointed out. "Didn't you ever read the prospectus? It says we're 'in the excellent care of Fairy Angora.' It wouldn't look very good for Silver Towers if we fell into an enchanted sleep for a hundred years."

That made us laugh—even Daisy—and as the coach began

bumping and rattling up a pretty, leafy lane, I decided I was really looking forward to meeting Witch Windlespin.

We finally stopped outside the sweetest little house nestled under a big oak tree. Fairy Angora was waiting by the tiny front door, and we tumbled out of the coach as fast as we could.

"Be sure to watch your heads as you go in," she warned us. "Listen very carefully, and don't be surprised by anything you see." She pushed the door open, and we tiptoed inside.

It was extraordinary! The door was so small, but the moment we were inside, we found ourselves in an enormous room, with a wonderful ceiling painted with sparkly stars and fat rosy cherubs holding trumpets and puffing out their cheeks. And then I saw there were little ships sailing in between the stars, and they were really moving, and the cherubs were making a game of blowing them this way and that—I'd never seen anything like it!

I was so busy staring up at the ceiling that I jumped when something touched my arm.

"Oh! Excuse me!" I said, and found I was talking to a broom!

And it actually bowed to me! I was so astonished I couldn't say anything at all.

"I see my broom has taken a fancy to you, dear Princess Katie," said a wonderfully deep voice, and

I saw Witch Windlespin smiling at me.

She was tall, and although she wasn't exactly beautiful she had the kindest, wisest face, and I suddenly knew she was very, very, *very* old.

She was dressed in a glorious shimmering gold silk gown with a fringed emerald green shawl around her shoulders, and there were golden lilies shining in her hair.

"Welcome to you and all your friends," she said. "This is my home. Please come and sit down."

The cottage was one of the most amazing places I've ever been.

There was a roaring fire, and in front of the fireplace were heaps and heaps of the softest rainbow-colored cushions and plush wool rugs and blankets. The students from the first coach were already sitting there looking so cozy, and a little black kitten was curled up on Princess Lisa's knees!

The six of us found our way to a heap of plumped-up indigo and purple pillows, and we sank into them as if we were settling into a heap of clouds. I don't think I've ever felt so cozy. I laid back and watched the cherubs blowing the ships. It was absolutely heavenly.

I could feel my eyelids drooping when suddenly there was an incredibly loud knock on the door.

Witch Windlespin had been arranging some pots and bottles on a table, and she looked up in surprise. "Goodness! I thought Fairy Angora was still outside. Princess Katie, would you let them in?"

Of course, I jumped up and hurried to the door. At once Gruella and Diamonde came barging past me, pushing the door open wide.

Chapter Three

The twins paused once they were inside and looked around the room rudely.

"Well!" Diamonde said in her rudest voice. "So *this* is a witch's house! Imagine!"

Gruella tipped her head to one

side. "I just don't know what Mommy would say if she saw us here."

Instead of being angry, Witch Windlespin gave the twins a beautiful smile. "I knew your great

grandmother, my dears, Queen Ethelberta. She was a very good friend of mine, and I'm so pleased to meet you. Do sit down."

Gruella and Diamonde didn't know what to do. They made a

noise like a balloon losing its air, and sat down with a flump. I caught Alice's eye, and I knew she was trying not to laugh.

The rest of our class followed the twins through the door, and then Fairy Angora appeared, looking hot and bothered.

"I'm so sorry," she said. "I left Lady Albina's lists in the coach, and I had to run and get them. She'd be so angry if I forgot them."

Witch Windlespin waved Fairy Angora over to a comfortable armchair. As she sat down to take attendance, the little black kitten jumped on her lap and started purring loudly.

"Just rest, Angora," Witch Windlespin said. "I'm going to show the princesses how I make a delicious potion for soothing away anxiety and fear. Now, who shall I have help me?"

She seemed to be looking at Daisy, and I knew Daisy would be really nervous if she were chosen, so I quickly raised my hand.

"Thank you, Princess Katie. Please come and join me."

I did feel a little bit anxious as I walked over to the table covered with exotic-looking jars and bottles, but I needn't have worried. It was so easy! I read out the names of the different herbs, and Witch Windlespin stirred them into a big silver bowl. It wasn't long before a wonderful smell began to fill the air.

"One final ingredient," said Witch Windlespin at last.

I read, "Essence of purest pine," and Witch Windlespin poured a beaker of golden liquid into the

bowl with a flourish. At once a burst of tiny stars flew out with a *fizz*.

"There!" Witch Windlespin poured the potion into a crystal bottle and held it up so we could see how wonderfully clear and sparkly it was. "Perfect! And now, just for fun, why don't some of you try, so you can see just how simple these potions are? Katie, let's see what you can do . . . . and Charlotte . . . Sophia . . . Diamonde . . . Emily . . . Daisy . . . Alice . . . oh, and Gruella."

My friends got up at once and came to join me by Witch Windlespin's little table. For a wonderful moment, I thought Diamonde and Gruella weren't going to come, but the broom whisked behind them and gently pushed them forward.

"Imagine us making a potion,

Gruella!" Diamonde said in her loudest voice.

"It looks exactly the same as cooking to me," Gruella smirked, "and Mommy always asks us to tell the cooks what to do, doesn't she, Diamonde?"

I thought Witch Windlespin might tell them off for being so boastful, but she didn't say anything. She fetched a clean bowl and put it down among the herbs and oils.

"Take your time," she said quietly, "and try to think peaceful thoughts

as you mix and blend the herbs. Remember, your innermost wishes may well be revealed in the potion you make, so do be careful!"

She smiled and drifted away to show the other princesses her dried flowers and the plants she used for dyeing her wools.

Chapter Four

*I*t had looked so easy when Witch Windlespin did it, but it was really hard when we tried. All the herbs got mixed up, and Gruella and Diamonde grabbed for the same bottle of oil and it spilled everywhere.

Diamonde tried to stir the mixture too fast, and it slopped over the edge of the bowl, and the strangest smell drifted up into the air. Gruella knocked a basket of lavender onto the floor, and I was certain we were going to end up with a terrible mess.

"Do you think we should tell Witch Windlespin we can't do it?" I asked.

To my surprise, Daisy shook her head. "Why don't we try again?" she suggested.

Alice said, "Yes!" and so did Sophia.

Emily, Daisy, and Charlotte nodded.

Diamonde and Gruella folded their arms and glared. "*We* don't want to start again," Gruella said.

The broom suddenly hopped forward and swept up the lavender. Then it skipped onto the table and,

in no time at all, the herbs were in neat piles and the oil stains were gone.

"Thank you!" I said, surprised.

"Oh, thank you so much!"

The broom bobbed a little bow, and leaned itself against the wall.

"Let's try again," Alice said. "I'm sure we could get it right if we try!"

The broom seemed to nod encouragingly, and we all laughed. Diamonde and Gruella pretended they hadn't seen it.

"Come on, then," I said, and Alice and Charlotte mixed up the herbs, Emily and Sophia poured in the oils, and Daisy and I stirred the mixture. When it was Daisy's turn, she stirred it very carefully with her eyes tightly shut.

"I'm trying to think peaceful

thoughts," she explained.

I was glad she was, because I was boiling inside. Gruella and Diamonde hadn't offered to help even once. I looked at them as I stirred, and I nearly said something mean. I actually had to bite my tongue. Inside my head I was wishing and wishing they weren't there. *If only they'd go away*, I thought, *the rest of us would have such a fabulous time*. But I didn't say anything. Then, the absolute minute we'd finished, *they* were the ones who raised their hands.

"Witch Windlespin," Gruella called out, and she sounded so

angelic, "we've finished! We've made the potion!"

"That's right," Diamonde said, and she gave me an icy stare. "And we did every bit of it all by ourselves."

If Witch Windlespin noticed me glaring at the twins, she didn't say anything. She picked up the bowl and held it to her nose with her eyes half shut.

"Hmmmm," she said thoughtfully. As she put the potion down,

the little black kitten jumped off
Fairy Angora's lap and came running
to see what we were doing. It
brushed against my leg and made
me jump, and I knocked into the
table. The bowl wobbled and half
the contents splashed over the

broom—and the broom *vanished*!

Everybody gasped except for me.

I knew whose fault it was that the broom had disappeared.

Mine.

I'd been wishing so hard that Gruella and Diamonde would go away that my thoughts had gotten mixed into our potion, and I'd made some *bad* magic.

Chapter Five

I didn't know what to do. Even Witch Windlespin was looking shocked.

"Goodness," she said. "I didn't expect that to happen. And my best broom too!" She turned to Gruella and Diamonde. "May I ask what you were thinking when you made this?"

If I hadn't been feeling so utterly and completely dreadful, I'd have laughed. Gruella turned yellow, and Diamonde turned red, and they both opened and shut their

mouths like goldfish.

Witch Windlespin looked at the potion and frowned.

"It's beautifully made," she said, "but there's something very wrong."

A sudden wild idea hit me. If I disappeared and went after the broom, maybe I could bring it back.

"Please," I said, "please, this is all my fault"—and I shut my eyes tight and plunged my hand into the bowl.

I waited to disappear, but nothing happened.

I just started sneezing and sneezing and sneezing, and I didn't think I'd ever be able to stop. And then Gruella and Diamonde started sneezing too, and they sneezed so hard that everything flew off the table except the bowl of magic potion. Herbs scattered everywhere and bottles crashed to the floor. You've never seen such a mess!

Fairy Angora came hurrying out

of her chair, but Witch Windlespin held up her hand.

"Let them sneeze their wishes away!" she commanded, and the three of us sneezed and sneezed, until gradually I stopped, and then Gruella stopped, and finally Diamonde stopped too.

"I really am very, very sorry," I whispered. "Will your broom ever come back?"

"See for yourself," said Witch Windlespin as she pointed at the wall.

At first I couldn't see anything, but all of a sudden I saw bristles, and then the handle, and there was the broom!

"Oh!" I was so pleased to see it again, I curtsied to it. "I'm so sorry I made you disappear!"

The broom gave a little hop and a skip.

"There," Witch Windlespin said. "No harm done."

"But what happened?" Fairy Angora asked. Witch Windlespin looked straight at me, and I knew what I had to do. I curtsied to the two grown-ups. Then I took a deep breath and curtsied to Gruella and Diamonde as well.

"I'm truly sorry," I said. "I was wishing that Gruella and Diamonde weren't here." I swallowed hard. "I know I'm very lucky to have my five special friends, and I do know I should be happy when other princesses join in with us,

but . . . but I failed."

"Thank you, Katie," said Witch Windlespin. "And now, Princess Gruella and Princess Diamonde, what have you got to say?"

I was sure the twins would say it wasn't their fault, but I was wrong.

Gruella gave a sort of gulp and

said, "I'm sorry too."

"Gruella!" Diamonde was horrified, but Gruella went on to say, "I was wishing Katie wasn't here. You were too, Diamonde, you know you were! She's so good at everything and she was so kind to Daisy, and"—two huge tears rolled down Gruella's cheeks—"it makes everyone love her and nobody ever loves me!"

And she began to cry.

Can you guess what I did next?

I hugged Gruella.

Does that sound odd? But she looked so miserable, I couldn't help it.

Then Diamonde said, "I suppose I'm sorry too." It didn't sound like she really meant it, but Witch Windlespin smiled, as if she believed every word.

"Good," she said. "And now let's look at the potion!"

We crowded around the table to look, and it was as clear and sparkling as the mixture Witch Windlespin had made.

"Excellent!" she said. "Don't you think, Fairy Angora, that these princesses have done well?"

Fairy Angora looked at us proudly. "Yes!" she said. "Ten tiara points each."

"But we don't deserve them!" Gruella burst out.

"Gruella dear, you've learned something much more important than how to make a potion," Witch Windlespin told her. Gruella looked so happy she positively glowed! Diamonde was staring glumly at the floor, but she gave a little nod.

"Right!" Witch Windlespin sounded brisk. "Now, let's have some fun! Katie, would you ask the broom to tidy up?"

Chapter Six

I turned to look at the broom, and it gave a couple of twirls and bowed a deep bow to me. I curtsied back.

"Please, dear broom," I said, "would you tidy up?"

At once the broom went crazy! It

whizzed around, piling the cushions on one side of the room, and it whisked away the table and tidied the pots and bottles onto a shelf, and the room was spotlessly clean and neat!

Witch Windlespin clapped her hands, and—oh!—it was so amazing! The rosy-cheeked cherubs on the ceiling put their trumpets to their lips and began to play. It was such catchy music, we couldn't help but start dancing. Even the kitten began prancing around! I did a little waltz with the broom, and I was about to grab Alice when a thought struck me.

I curtsied my very best curtsy to Gruella. "Would Your Majesty do me the honor of dancing with me?"

Gruella curtsied back. "It would be my pleasure," she said, and off we went, around and around and

around the room until we were dizzy and had to stop.

At exactly that moment, the front door flew open, and a shower of twinkly stars drifted down from the ceiling. In came Prince Dandino,

beaming from ear to ear, and
behind him came a trail of little
pageboys carrying boxes and boxes
of the most delicious royal pizza.

We scurried to sit on the rainbow cushions for a pizza party. It was so much fun! We all chatted and laughed, and the cherubs played softer, sweeter music, and it was magical.

As the carriages rolled away from Witch Windlespin's house late that afternoon, I gave a huge happy sigh.

"Wasn't it a wonderful day?" I said.

"It was amazing," Daisy agreed, and then she grinned at me. "And I wasn't frightened, not once."

"It must have been Witch Windlespin's potion for soothing away anxiety and fear," Charlotte said sleepily.

"No it wasn't," Daisy told her.

"It was having all of you to take care of me. Especially Katie!"

"We take care of one another," I said, and it was true. My friends were just the very best ever, and I was so lucky to be at Silver Towers, and I'm so very, very glad you're here with us too.

What happens next?

FIND OUT IN

Princess Daisy
∽ AND THE ∽
Magical Merry-Go-Round

Hello! I'm Daisy. Princess Daisy.
And I do hope you're enjoying
being at Silver Towers with
us. You're exactly the right
kind of princess, you know—
just like my lovely friends,
Charlotte, Katie, Alice, Sophia, and Emily.

And not at all like Diamonde and
Gruella—they're so stuck up.

Do you get nervous before you do something new? I do. I try so hard not to, but I
can't help it. And learning to be a Perfect
Princess means we're always doing new
things or going to new places. . . .

You are cordially invited
to the Royal Princess Academy

**Follow the adventures of your special princess friends
as they try to earn enough points to join the Tiara Club.**

Katherine Tegen Books
An Imprint of HarperCollinsPublishers